Meet the Stars of

ROSWELL

An Unauthorized Biography

By Samantha Calderone

SCHOLASTIC INC.

NEW YORK TORONTO LONDON AUCKLAND SYDNEY
MEXICO CITY NEW DELHI HONG KONG

This unofficial biography is not authorized by or affiliated with the producers or stars of *Roswell*.

ISBN 0-439-20758-4

Cover and insert designed by Madalina Stefan

12 11 10 9 8 7 6 5 4 3 2 1   0 1 2 3 4 5 6/0

Printed in the U.S.A.
First Scholastic printing, July 2000

ROSWELL'S REALITY

In the summer of 1999, before it debuted, *Roswell* was already one of the most talked about new dramas of the upcoming fall television season. For starters, it featured an easy to look at ensemble cast portraying the teens of Roswell High School. But what set it a notch above other teen shows was its premise that three of the leading characters — Max, Michael, and Isabel — were survivors of the purported July 1947 UFO crash. That's right, teenage aliens.

All the trio know about their past is that they emerged from incubation pods when they were six years old. They assumed "normal" human form, were adopted by local families, and assimilated into the American culture.

Now, not unlike other teens trying to find *their* place in the world, aliens Max Evans, his sister Isabel, and their friend Michael

Guerin are struggling to find out who they are. But they really need to know where they come from, if there are others out there like them, and who their real parents are. It's a constant balancing act to try to "fit in" at their Roswell, New Mexico, high school and allay suspicions at home while searching for answers. So *Roswell* isn't just about normal teen angst, it's a genuine case of teen alienation.

The very first episode set the tone. It also spilled some major secrets. It opened at the local diner — the Crashdown Cafe. A fight broke out between two customers and shots were fired. One of 'em nailed waitress Liz Parker. She fell to the ground and should have been a goner, but minutes later got up, pretty much without a scratch.

Max Evans had come to her rescue. Using paranormal powers, Max gently placed his hand upon Liz's wound — and *presto!* the wound healed itself. Lucky for Liz, her life was spared. Not the brightest move for Max, whose secret came awfully close to being exposed.

Close enough to arouse the suspicions of

the already distrustful Sheriff Valenti. And close enough for Max to eventually be forced to confess all to Liz. "I'm not from around here," he told her in that first episode, pointing to the sky as she wonders aloud where his home really is.

Unsurprisingly, *that* set off a chain of events. Liz told her best friend Maria, who first freaked out, then blabbed to her friend Alex. Meanwhile, Max told Michael and his sister Isabel that he told Liz — and that she told Maria, etc. So that made six who knew, and who vowed to keep the secret.

Intertwined with the suspenseful overtones are the romantic moments between Max and Liz, and later Michael and Maria. That, naturally, comes with its own set of complications. Liz used to date Kyle, until the Crashdown Cafe incident when she fell for Max. As for Max, he never had feelings for anyone before Liz came along. The two seem to be a perfect pair — if interspecies dating works out! Same goes for Michael and Maria, who are totally into each other — but know they shouldn't be.

Roswell is as much about the aliens unlocking clues to their past as it is about defining their future. Will Max, Isabel, and Michael ever find their way home? Will Max and Liz ever really get together? Will Sheriff Valenti discover the teens' secret? And if he does, what will he do? The only people who know are *Roswell*'s creative production team, and they're not saying. Read on to find out how *Roswell* became a reality in our universe.

THE BACKSTORY

Producer Jason Katims has long been a fan of relationship dramas. With credits like *My So-Called Life* and *Relativity* under his belt, Jason was looking for his next project when he stumbled upon the Roswell High book series by author Melinda Metz. He soon was hooked, especially intrigued with the romantic undercurrent between Liz and Max.

"When I read the novel that the series is based on, there were a lot of things that were appealing about it," Jason explained to TV critics. "It was a love story with a real obstacle to it and I think a lot of writers are continually drawn to wanting to write a Romeo and Juliet–type love story, a story with a real obstacle. And I think that the fact that Liz and Max are different life-forms gives you a *real* obstacle."

To make his idea a reality, Jason hooked up with *X-Files* producer David Nutter and Jonathan Frakes of *Star Trek: The Next Generation* fame. Originally the show was supposed to air on the Fox network. But there were all sorts of glitches — in the end, *Roswell* found its home on the teen-friendly WB network. The show was picked up for an entire season — twenty-two episodes. Traditionally, new shows are contracted for thirteen episodes. That is, they are given that half a season chance to prove themselves, find an audience, and if successful, they are picked up for what's known as "the back nine."

Jason Katims concludes, "To me, one of the exciting things about the premise of the show is that the three alien characters in the show don't know about their history, which makes — from a writing point of view — it exciting because as they discover their backstory, the audience is discovering it. So it's something that we're going to discover with them, and it will be a long ride and hopefully a really fulfilling journey."

Now, read on to meet the talented cast of young actors who inhabit *Roswell*.

MEET JASON BEHR

MAX EVANS

Max Evans has a heart of gold. He wouldn't hurt anyone. In fact, you could *almost* say he cares to a fault. When he witnessed the girl of his dreams, Liz Parker, shot in the Crashdown Cafe one afternoon, he used his secret powers in public to save her. He didn't stop to think about the risk *he* was taking!

Obviously Max wants to share all his secrets with Liz, but the handsome, vulnerable sixteen-year-old isn't completely sure what they are himself. He's curious about his past and worried about his future. So Max, his alien sister Isabel, and their friend Michael Guerin continue to explore their roots while dodging the suspicious, ever-present Sheriff Valenti. Although Max longs to find out where he came from and if he has any "real" family, he is very happy with his adoptive parents. He's a good student at Roswell High School and a good son and brother at home.

Like Max Evans, the actor who plays him, Jason Behr is a gentle soul. When he's working, he gives his all to the performance and to his fellow actors, and when he's not working, he's a loyal, caring friend. These personal attributes of Jason's helped him land the role of Max. He's glad he did. Jason enthuses, "Max is by far the most interesting character I've played. All of the different layers and dimensions to him and the way he deals with relationships is a lot of fun to discover."

"HE'S ALWAYS BEEN VERY ARTISTIC"

Jason was born in Minneapolis, Minnesota, and raised in the suburb of Richfield. He grew up in a single-parent home after his parents' divorce. His childhood friend Jenny Reher says her longtime pal was showing signs of individuality well before anyone else in their St. Richard's elementary school class. "We went to a small private school where our class didn't have much more than twenty kids in the entire grade. We had to wear a uniform, but Jason always had ways to have fun with it, while staying within the rules. He always had watches or things that were a little bit different from the rest of us. We were always clueless when it came to fashion because we always wore navy blue and white. The boys could get by with navy slacks and white cotton shirts. If he could get by with wearing a navy sweatshirt of some brand, like Guess?, he would do it. He wore Swatch watches — those were really cool then — and I think he had almost every one. He was so much more up on everything than we were, we just looked to him for style."

In addition to his early fashion sensibilities, Jason was also creative. "He's always been very artistic," Jenny says. "He's very talented. He would do *projects*. When most kids were doing stick figures, he was doing detailings. In 1984 there was a coloring contest for our city. We had to come up with a theme and then we drew pictures. 'Let Your Feelings Soar in 1984' was the theme. He did a bald eagle and he got recognition for that. He and I rode on a float together because we both won the coloring contest."

Jason's talents extended beyond the page and onto the stage. Encouraged by his mom, he appeared in his first school play when he was five. He was a natural, Jenny says. "We kind of got to vote who got to play the different parts. For the big part we would all say Jason should because it had the most lines. We did that because we knew he knew how to do it."

The experience was fun for the wide-eyed half-pint, who was developing a fascination for television and movies. All he could think about was wanting to do it again. Jason told the *Washington Times,* "Acting seemed natural and fun to me, and the whole family supported everything I did. My mother was always there, but never threw me into anything that I did not initiate. Her attitude was always, 'Whatever you want to do, Jason.'"

A CBS holiday movie, *A Season's Greeting,* chose the snowy, seasonally compliant Minnesota as a shooting location. Jason was six and after a tryout was chosen to play one of several children gathered for a Christmas caroling scene. It was his professional acting debut. "I don't remember much of it except bitter cold and snowstorms," he says. "I was singing 'We Wish You a Merry Christmas' with three other kids on the back of a horse-drawn sleigh. I thought the guy in the beard and fuzzy hat was Abraham Lincoln," Jason recalled to the *Times* reporter.

While shooting a movie outdoors was a bummer, the exposure to "Lights, camera, action!" was a thrill. Little Jason continued to be on the lookout for more acting gigs. When he was eight, he landed a plum spot in a Stomper Trucks toy commercial, also filmed in Minneapolis. Along with building his acting career, Jason did some modeling for local department stores. Not only did talent agencies find Jason's looks appealing, so did his young female classmates. "Our class size was very small when we were young, and there were, like, ten girls in the class and at least five of them had a crush on him," Jenny recalls.

HOTTIE IN THE MAKING

When Jason reached junior high school, he was able to shed the navy blue and white school uniforms of his private elementary school and wear pretty much what he wanted in public school. Jenny says, "At that point his [style] influence got even bigger. I remember he always had a lock of hair over one eye, like a thrasher, skateboarder thing. He wore big sweatshirts and jeans that were kind of baggy, cool floppy shoes like the old-style Converse Chuck Taylors. Most of us were clueless watching Jason be totally New York, totally trendsetting, and doing things."

The 1988 Richfield Junior High yearbook featured a skateboarding theme. Jason, an avid skateboarder, was photographed extensively for the yearbook's black-and-white pages. Wearing the baggy sweatshirt and jeans and sneakers that Jenny describes, Jason is seen in several photos, performing different jumps and tricks on his skateboard. Even back then, he was a natural in front of a camera.

Jason's looks may have caught the eye of many young female admirers, but it was his winning personality that made him popular with *everybody* — classmates and teachers alike. "He was in the popular group, but he was friends with everybody. He had that kind of mentality," Jenny says. "He was always such a clown. One of our sixth-grade teachers said that he was an actor, a model, a comedian. He was always joking around, pulling pranks, but not anything harmful. He always had a good heart. The teachers really liked him."

Still, he had insecurities. "I was a shrimp compared to the rest of my friends," Jason described. "I was short and I don't think I grew until I was in eleventh grade. I felt like every other teenager feels, a little out of place and lost."

Maybe so, but his classmates and teachers remember Jason as very focused on what he wanted. And at Richfield High School, Jason came into his own. He stood nearly six feet tall, and his naturally athletic build developed an extra layer of muscles. He wasn't a member of any of Richfield's athletic teams, but he was very active in afterschool intramural softball, basketball, football, and broomball, which is like ice hockey played with broomsticks.

Jenny says Jason had a knack for making everyone feel included. "He was always organizing activities. He was the captain of the broomball team, which plays the faculty. It was always so fun, and his team often won. It's kind of a big deal because the whole school comes and it's always fun to see the teachers out there slipping and sliding on the ice."

Jenny continues, "He never had to be the captain of the football team to be popular. He was always one of those people who was involved and social. He wasn't one to go to parties where people were drinking and stuff like that. His philosophy was basically to have fun, no enemies."

In keeping with that philosophy, Jason

and some friends, Jenny recalls, "organized a barbecue crew. In eleventh or twelfth grade before every football game they would go outside and grill in the parking lot. It was Jason and eight or ten guys, but of course they'd invite whoever wanted to come."

Jason was very involved with other school activities as well. He was a member of the Aurean yearbook staff during his senior year, and he participated with philanthropic groups P3 (they called it P-cubed), which stood for Positive Peer Pressure, and SADD, Students Against Driving Drunk. Members of these groups, Jenny explains, made "a commitment to stay away from alcohol, chemicals, and be tobacco free and to encourage other people to do the same."

DESTINED FOR FAME

Jason remained committed to his schoolwork, his friends, but most of all his passion for acting. Debra Holman, Dean of Students at Richfield High School and yearbook adviser, recalls that Jason's ambitions as a teenager were always clear. "He definitely talked about acting in high school. By that time, he had done a lot of commercials and modeling. But he was not at all arrogant about it. People respected him for what he did, but he didn't brag about it. If I wanted to know anything, I had to ask him. So we weren't surprised that he went to Los Angeles to make it. We kind of expected it."

Jason displayed several key qualities when he was a senior that would serve him well in his pursuit of professional acting. Ms. Holman says, "He was conscientious and hardworking. In the field that he's in there's going to be a lot of times when he's going to have rejection. He went for what he wanted in spite of the setbacks. He was very focused."

When Jason graduated in 1992, his Richfield senior class — approximately four hundred students — voted him "Most Destined for Fame." "He was a superstar from the time we were very young," Jenny concluded. "We knew he'd make it."

Jason had saved his money and, not long after he graduated, made his plan to move to California. A friend from junior high was living in Los Angeles and told Jason he could crash at his place. So he packed up his belongings, said good-bye to his family and friends, and jumped on a Hollywood-bound plane.

It was a struggle at first because he only landed sporadic commercial work, but Jason persevered. In 1994, Jason won a guest-starring role on the TV comedy *Step By Step*. His big breakthrough came the following year, when he landed a regular role on the critically acclaimed Showtime series *Sherman Oaks*. Jason's acting "dance card" soon began to fill up with more episodic work on *Pacific Blue*, *Buffy the Vampire Slayer*, *JAG*, *Profiler*, and *7th Heaven*.

Then, in 1998, Jason was cast as track star Dempsey Easton in the short-lived ABC series *Push*, a drama about athletes in pursuit of Olympic gold. The show was panned by the critics and only aired four times before being yanked from the schedule. It was pretty frustrating for Jason and the cast, who had all trained for months to make their portrayals realistic. Actress Maureen Flannigan, who played swimmer Erin Galway, explains, "We had to train like maniacs, not like athletes, like maniacs! We started production in January '98, but we actually began training in October '97. It was like strict diets, working out five days a week. It was like boot camp for all of us."

But Jason wasn't out of work for long. Later that year he filmed a small part in the feature film *Pleasantville* and then landed a recurring role on the ever-popular *Dawson's Creek.* He played high schooler Chris Wolfe, a friend of the not-so-nice (and eventually doomed) Abby. The gig was like a dream come true. "I was really nervous when I went down there," Jason recalls of his first days on *Dawson's* Wilmington, North Carolina, set. "They were all established as a group, and it was a little awkward being the new guy. But right after I got into town Kerr Smith [Jack] called and invited me to go shoot pool and hang out. I instantly felt at ease."

Jason had a lot of fun with the *Dawson's*

gang, but in early 1999 his agent called to tell him about *Roswell*. It was the kind of chance most actors only dream of — a lead role on a television show. And Jason immediately knew it was a project he didn't want to pass up. So he bid good-bye to his friends in North Carolina and headed back to Los Angeles to try out for *Roswell*. He won the role of Max hands down and has loved every minute of it.

Jason's fans can't wait to see what comes next. Since *Roswell*'s debut, he's been a star on the rise. *TV Guide* put him on their "Ten to Watch" list in November 1999, and magazines clamor for interviews. But all of the press attention hasn't affected Jason, who still prefers family over the Hollywood party scene. He hasn't forgotten where he came from. "Whenever he's in town he makes an effort to see people," says Ms. Holman, noting that several press clippings on Jason have made the Richfield High bulletin board. "The fact that he does come back and see his friends here — I think it says a lot that he hasn't outgrown his Richfield friends."

BEHR ESSENTIALS

REAL NAME: Jason Nathaniel Behr

HOW YOU SAY IT: Bear

BIRTHDAY: December 30, 1973

ASTROLOGICAL SIGN: Capricorn

BIRTHPLACE: Minneapolis, Minnesota

RAISED IN: Richfield, Minnesota

FAMILY: Mom, Patricia
Three brothers, Andrew, John, and Aaron

EDUCATION: Graduated from
Richfield High School in 1992

WE KNEW IT: Jason was voted "Most
Destined for Fame" by his graduating class

PETS: Dog, Ronin, an Akita

FOOD INDULGENCE: Krispy Kreme donuts

HOBBIES: Hiking with Ronin,
playing basketball with friends

FAVORITE BAND: The Dave Matthews
Band

FAVORITE MOVIE: *The Godfather*

FAVORITE ACTOR: Paul Newman

UPCOMING PROJECT: *Rites of Passage,*
an independent film

MEET SHIRI APPLEBY

LIZ PARKER

Liz Parker is the ultimate all-American girl. She's a good student at Roswell High, a good friend, has a good job at the Crashdown Cafe, and has the admiration of not one but *two* of Roswell's teen hotties. One is an alien named Max, and the other is Kyle, who sometimes feels alienated by Liz.

She's sweet and shy and very much smitten with Max, who brought her back to life after a gunshot wound nearly killed her. Liz is a hopeless romantic whose heart longs for the deep connection Max provides.

Her relationship with Kyle cooled considerably after she met Max. However, Liz remains cordial to Kyle in an effort to allay the suspicions his father, Sheriff Valenti, harbors about the circumstances surrounding the Crashdown shooting. Meantime,

Max, wary of all of the suspicion surrounding him, asks that Liz be an understanding friend — and nothing more. Her heart yearns for Max, but her head tells her that just being friends is the right thing to do.

Shiri Appleby certainly hasn't had any alien encounters in real life, but she says she can totally relate to Liz Parker's high school existence. "I've had the same group of friends since I was in the first grade. It's funny, but this isn't really a stretch for me to play a teenager, since high school was, like, two years ago for me."

What else does Shiri have in common with Liz? "We look alike," she giggles. "I've always kept a journal. Well, I've gone in and out at times of having one, but most of the time I do keep one. You've got to write down your thoughts and express things."

When Shiri first read the *Roswell* script, she was immediately drawn to the complexity of the aliens' situation and the overriding love story between Max and Liz. "The character carries herself with a lot of respect and dignity, but at the same time she's just as scared and confused as any teenager growing up," Shiri says. "I'm sure there are a lot of people going through the same problems, so they can relate."

CALIFORNIA GIRL, TAKE ONE

Shiri was born on December 7, 1978, in Calabasas, California, which is approximately twenty miles north of the bright lights of Hollywood. The affluent community is known for its spacious homes, rolling hills, and blue skies. Her name, Shiri, means "my song" in Hebrew. Like many young girls who grow up in sunny Southern California, Shiri took an interest in modeling and acting at an early age. It wasn't because her parents encouraged her to do it, she just wanted to. "Neither of my parents was in the business," Shiri explains. "It was just sort of my thing I wanted to try. My brother had soccer and I did acting."

The dark-haired, brown-eyed beauty thought it would be fun to try on clothes and smile for the cameras, maybe say a few lines. And her parents, Dena and Jerry, agreed. "I started acting when I was four years old," Shiri says. "I took a big interest in it and my parents were very supportive. I started out in commercials and guest appearances in television shows. The first thing I did was a Raisin Bran commercial!"

Shiri downed a lot of cereal that day, but sadly for her, the commercial never ran. Still, she forged ahead with more work in commercials for Cheerios, M&M's, and Taco Bell, until she landed a recurring role on the soap opera *Santa Barbara*. She began the arduous routine of being a kid actor, balancing her schoolwork with her acting. It went as follows: "I'd get up in the morning, go to work, bring my homework to the studio teacher, do three hours on the set, go home, do more homework, go to bed, then go to school the next day."

Her schedule was tough but not unheard of. Because it was Los Angeles, there were other kids who acted at her school. "It wasn't abnormal at all. It was like, 'That's the girl from that show.' It wasn't a big deal."

Throughout elementary and junior high

school, Shiri's acting credits continued to build. She appeared in TV movies like *The Story of a Mafia Wife* and *Go Toward the Light*. Then, in 1990, Shiri got a big break, landing a role in the movie comedy *I Love You to Death*, which starred Kevin Kline, Tracey Ullman, and Keanu Reeves.

From that point on, Shiri continued to do a slew of television guest spots on popular shows like *thirtysomething* and *Doogie Howser, M.D.* Of the latter experience, Shiri says with a giggle, "I played this girl in the hospital who had a big crush on Doogie."

There was more. Shiri guested on *ER*, the short-lived television series *Knight and Daye*, and *Sunday Dinner*, and TV films *Perfect Family* and *Family Prayers*. All of the work kept Shiri and her mom, Dena, very busy shuttling back and forth between home and the studios. At an age when most young girls are trying to distance themselves from their parents, Shiri and her mother actually became closer. "The times when my mom went to auditions and we spent time going back and forth talking," Shiri explains, "it wasn't the auditions, it was great just getting to be with her. And hopefully I'll grow up like her and be able to discuss everything. I hope we never have a wall of communication between us."

"I KIND OF DROPPED OUT OF THE BUSINESS"

A funny thing happened when Shiri entered her teens — she began to long for a "normal" teen life. While she was juggling her burgeoning acting career and her algebra homework, her friends were going shopping after school, attending student council meetings, working at part-time jobs, just being teenagers. That looked really appealing — so she took a break. "I kind of dropped out of the business for about three years and just spent time being a normal teenager," Shiri explains. "I just didn't want anything to interfere with school or my friends. I didn't want to miss out on anything and regret it."

Hollywood's loss was Calabasas High School's gain, where Shiri was a model student. For two years she served as the yearbook editor. "I was pretty involved, on lots of committees and stuff." And stuff? Sheepishly, Shiri admits, "I was a cheerleader."

Shiri talked on the phone with her friends, attended school football games, and — like Liz Parker — waitressed. She worked part-time at the local California Pizza Kitchen, earning a mere fraction of what her acting jobs used to pay. But, Shiri says, she was richer for the experience. "It was a lot of fun, plus it helps now when I have to do a scene in the cafe and carry things," Shiri giggles.

Upon graduating in 1996, Shiri, voted "Most Spirited" by her class, enrolled at the University of Southern California to study English. "I moved into my own place and I thought college was what I wanted. But then I just kept thinking that I really missed acting, so I started auditioning again. I didn't drop out, I'm taking a leave of absence. I have ten years to go back. I'll go back. But not right away. We work, like, seventeen hours a day, it's exhausting. By the time I get home, I couldn't imagine having to stay up and write a term paper. School alone is so hard."

CALIFORNIA GIRL, TAKE TWO

It didn't take Shiri long to get back into the swing of things. Soon after she started auditioning, she landed guest spots on *Xena: Warrior Princess, Beverly Hills, 90210,* and *7th Heaven,* and a small part in a film titled *The 13th Floor.*

When *Roswell* was casting in early 1999, Shiri immediately wanted to go for the role of Liz. One problem — she was having trouble getting an audition. But just as Shiri was about to give up hope, a friend of hers came along with an idea. This friend knew the show's creator, David Nutter, and offered to pass along Shiri's photo and resume. Shiri reluctantly agreed. "I wasn't sure that was the way to go. I felt like it was a little like cheating," Shiri says.

But that was only the beginning. While the other roles were cast in one or two audition sessions, Shiri had to audition *eight times*! "I read for all three of the female parts," Shiri describes. "I think what really drew me was the writing. It really spoke to me and it is written in a really realistic way, so for people my age it is really easy to understand."

These days, Shiri is one happy girl. She's on a hit show, she's got a cool West Los Angeles apartment (and a new cat named Abby), and she gets to work side by side with hunky Jason Behr! "He is a wonder," Shiri gushes. "We have become very good friends and I really admire him. He really holds my hand through a lot of this stuff. He's very down-to-earth, which is nice. I've done a lot of acting in my life, but nothing like this. This is a new script every other week and the stories are so intense. It's so interesting to see where things are going."

Shiri hopes to be acting for many years to come. "It's the one thing I'm passionate about. I would love to be able to work for as long as I live." Her idol is the late Lucille Ball. "Lucille Ball could take any situation. She really broke a lot of boundaries for women and I think that's really respectable to go out and really take a chance. I really admire her."

SHIRI SHORTS

FULL NAME: ———————— Shiri Appleby

HOW YOU SAY IT: ———————— SHEAR-eee APPLE-bee

BIRTHDAY: ———————— December 7, 1978

ASTROLOGICAL SIGN: ———————— Sagittarius

BIRTHPLACE: ———————— Panorama City, California

RAISED IN: ———————— Calabasas, California

FAMILY: ———————— Mom, Dena, a teacher Dad, Jerry, a telecommunications executive Brother, Evan

EDUCATION: ———————— Graduated from Calabasas High School in 1996. Currently on leave of absence from the University of Southern California, where she's majoring in English

FIRST NONACTING JOB: ———————— Hostess at California Pizza Kitchen during high school

PETS: ———————— Cat, Abby, nicknamed Princess Pound Kitty because Shiri adopted her from a local animal shelter

HOBBIES:———————— Shopping, bike riding
along the beach, sleeping in
FAVORITE FOOD:———————————— Pasta
FAVORITE SNACK:———————Frozen Reese's Pieces
FAVORITE ACTRESS:———————— Lucille Ball
JUST READ:—— *Angela's Ashes* by Frank McCourt
and *Catcher in the Rye* by J. D. Salinger

MEET BRENDAN FEHR

MICHAEL GUERIN

Michael, who is best friends with Max and Isabel, has trouble relating to other people. When the three of them emerged from their incubation pods ten years ago, Michael was instinctively wary of this new world. The frightened little boy hid behind a rock while Max and Isabel joined hands and accepted their future. Lucky for them they ended up in a loving adoptive home. Not so for Michael.

Unlike Max and Isabel's situation, Michael's "family" doesn't sit down to dinner every night. His adoptive father is an alcoholic who lives in a trailer park and collects welfare checks. He's abusive to Michael and frankly couldn't care less about his son. Perhaps that's why Michael, much more so than Isabel and Max, is distrustful of others and longs to return to his real home. Wherever that may be.

Brendan Fehr has a difficult time relating to his tortured teenage alien alter ego, Michael Guerin. Michael's intense, brooding personality is the polar opposite of Brendan's. In fact, ask any member of the *Roswell* cast and they're likely to tell you that Brendan is one of the nicest, most outgoing people they've ever met. Brendan jokes that he's nothing like Michael because "I'm a real mama's boy."

NORTH OF THE BORDER

When Brendan was born, his parents and two older sisters were delighted to welcome a boy to their New Westminster, British Columbia, home. Like most Canadian kids, Brendan grew up a big fan of sports, especially ice hockey. In Canada, it's often said that young boys learn how to skate before they learn how to walk. And that's certainly the case with Brendan. He has enjoyed playing hockey since his early days in suburban Vancouver, just like fellow actors Jason Priestley and Michael J. Fox, who also hail from his hometown.

Academics were also stressed in the Fehr household, and Brendan didn't disappoint. He excelled in all of his school subjects, especially science and math. When Brendan looks back on his school days, he prefers to downplay his outstanding accomplishments. "I was a pretty good athlete. I played a lot of hockey, volleyball, football. Above average in most, but not spectacular in any."

But it was clear to Brendan's family, friends, and teachers that he could do anything he put his mind to. One thing Brendan couldn't do, however, was save his parents' marriage. When he was twelve, Brendan's folks split up, and he and his mother moved to Winnipeg, Manitoba, Canada. Brendan was sad to leave his father and his friends, but he soon adjusted to life in Winnipeg.

Brendan quickly made friends with fellow students and teachers at his new Winnipeg school, Mennonite Brethren Collegiate Institute. In contrast to the Roswell High that Michael Guerin attends, MBCI is a small private school located in suburban Winnipeg, the capital of Manitoba. Unlike other high schools, MBCI had no formal football team or hockey team. Approximately 560 kids, male and female, comprise the student body in grades seven through twelve. Brendan says, "I had eighty people in my graduating class."

As teacher Paul Doerksen explains, "We're a Christian private school. So we have chapel and required biblical studies courses and try as best we can to create certain atmospheres and promote certain values." Brendan, Mr. Doerksen explains, "certainly fit into the kind of a place that we're kind of trying to work at here. He wasn't a rebel or anything. He was almost always a positive influence in our school. I think it's fair to call him a relatively dynamic guy, in terms of the students who would want to be with him. You could see that in those days."

Mr. Doerksen continues, "I coached him in freshman volleyball and taught him Canadian history in grade eleven and religion in grade twelve. He was a very good student. In grade eleven he was promoted with first-class honors. First-class honors here is an average above ninety."

In fact, Brendan was such a good student and was so motivated and inspired by his teachers that he decided to go to college and become a teacher. "He was certainly talking about going to university," Mr. Doerksen says.

WORKER BEE

Talking about it was one thing — paying for college was another. Brendan's family was not wealthy, so he had to pay his own way. He did it via a couple of part time jobs. One was a summer job with a lawn care company called Eco Green. Brendan's job at Eco Green consisted of joining a crew of workers to go to specific residential and commercial sites and spray lawns with fertilizers and chemicals to keep them healthy. Because it's a seasonal business, Brendan and his fellow workers spent long hours on the job, usually from sunup to sundown. It was exhausting work that required a team effort from the employees to get the job done. Teamwork was a concept Brendan was familiar with, and he found the long hours and hard labor very rewarding.

He was, as his former boss Dillon Vincent says, "An employer's dream. He worked all summer with us. He enjoyed the work and even enjoyed that it was pretty long hours. When we first started our business we ran it out of our house, and I had a couple of small kids. At the end of working a long, hard day, Brendan would always take the time to push the kids on the swings and play around with them."

Like Mr. Doerksen, Mr. Vincent can't say enough nice things about Brendan. "Brendan was probably one of the best employees we ever had," his former boss gushes. "When he started with our company he was probably the youngest employee we ever had — he was only seventeen years old, but he really sort of took charge of things. Whenever we'd send a group of employees out to a commercial site where they were spraying a large area, Brendan would always sort of take charge of the situation and start directing one guy to spray one area and one guy to spray another area. He had really good judgment with making those calls."

Nobody resented Brendan's leadership skills. They respected him for his stringent work ethic. "He's just a supernice guy. He got along well with everybody. He always strove for improvement in his work. In the winters he worked for a company called Mat Master, and what they did was deliver floor mats. And in keeping with Brendan's whole attitude toward work he would go and deliver his quota of mats, and he'd always be sort of increasing the quota — and I'm not sure that the other employees always liked the fact that Brendan could always sort of outperform everybody. But then, just to help them out, if Brendan got finished with his route early at the mat business, he would go and deliver mats for some of his coworkers just to kind of help them along. If I could hire employees like Brendan every year I'd be thrilled. People like him just don't come along very often."

NEW BEGINNING

All the hard work, in high school and on the job, paid off. He graduated from MBCI in 1995 with first-class honors, having maintained above a ninety percent average in his high school studies. Brendan's teachers at MBCI were thrilled to learn that he'd been accepted to the University of Manitoba.

Mr. Doerksen says Brendan displayed "a certain kind of intelligence that includes a creative side, especially his writing." These skills made Brendan an ideal candidate for college, teaching, or whatever career he wanted to pursue. But acting? "I have to say that's not one of the categories when I think of 'What could my students turn into in the future?'" Mr. Doerksen says with a chuckle. "I tend not to think of them becoming actors.

I think more along conventional lines — historian, theologian. We try to stress service and people helping and that kind of thing as well. So we have those sorts of hopes for our students. Being a Hollywood star kind of doesn't come onto the screen much, eh?"

But during the summer of 1995, while Brendan was lunching with his pals at Eco Green, the subject of modeling came up. Brendan and his cohorts were intrigued that people actually got paid to put on new clothes and smile for the camera. "They were talking about modeling and Brendan said 'Oh, I could do that,'" Mr. Vincent explains.

So Brendan investigated what it would take to model in the Winnipeg area. He found out soon enough. "So for one of the grocery store chains, Super Store, he started modeling for some of their flyers. He really enjoyed that, and he thought, Wow, this is pretty good, easy money, just smiling and putting these clothes on," Mr. Vincent recalled.

The Super Store experience made Brendan curious about pursuing other modeling and acting jobs in Winnipeg. Even though he had no other previous experience, he decided to try. "Who doesn't want to be on TV once in their life, or have a chance at it?" Brendan says.

His bosses at Eco Green were impressed with Brendan's drive and always tried to accommodate his requests for time off. "There was a local movie that was being produced and Brendan was asking us 'Do you think I could get a few hours off if I get a role in this movie because I'd really like to give it a try?' And we said sure, we'll accommodate you any way we can," Mr. Vincent explains. "It was just a one hour type of movie and it was shot in Winnipeg on a pretty small budget. He'd come to work every day and give us a progress report as he started acting and he'd say 'This is really neat. I really enjoy doing this type of stuff.'"

"I WAS BASICALLY IN THE RIGHT PLACE AT THE RIGHT TIME"

At the end of the summer of 1997, Brendan was in Vancouver, British Columbia, for a friend's wedding. It was going to be his last trip of the summer — he was less than a week away from starting his freshman year at the University of Manitoba. Brendan decided that while he was in town he'd check out some of the local modeling and talent agencies. He walked into the offices of Look Talent, and his life changed in an instant. "My now manager, we met at his office, a flukish kind of thing, and he asked me one of those cheesy lines like, 'Do you want to be on TV?' And things just rolled from there," Brendan explains. "I was basically in the right place at the right time."

But Brendan was torn between pursuing acting and his undergraduate degree. So he asked his mother! She told him college could wait. "She encouraged me to do it, in the sense that if I was going to act, this was the time to do it. I read in one magazine that she encouraged me to drop out of college and go for it. No, I *had* to drop out of college to do it, but she didn't *encourage* me to drop out of college. I was nineteen at the time, and I was allowed to kind of veer off on a particular path and try something new, give a year of my life away just to have fun. And it turned into this."

Within weeks Brendan landed a steady stream of work, starting with a role in the Canadian television series *Breaker High*. Next up was a part in a high-profile ABC movie of the week, *Our Guys*, with Eric Stoltz and Ally Sheedy. Other credits included TV movies like *Perfect Little Angels* and *Every Mother's Worst Fear*, plus a guest-starring role in the TV series *Millennium*. Then Brendan was cast in a small role in the teen suspense thriller *Disturbing Behavior*, which was directed by one of *Roswell*'s creators, David Nutter.

ANYBODY NEED AN ALIEN?

Not long after, Brendan was asked to audition for the *Roswell* producers. "Originally I didn't want to try out for *Roswell*," Brendan confesses. "I didn't think it was going to be too good. You know, teenage aliens. I thought it could be kind of cheesy. [But then] I walked into the audition room and I saw David Nutter and I knew it would be good because I worked with him before." Brendan read first for the role of Max, *then* for Michael. "I was much more comfortable the second time reading for Michael. I thought he was a better character for me and I thought I could nail it."

And nail it he did. Brendan's approach to portraying Michael has captured Hollywood's attention and that of many newfound fans. "When I started off, I got one fan letter, from this one girl who kept writing me, 'I know you're getting lots of fan mail,'" Brendan explains. "And she was the *only* one writing."

Brendan's fan mail has increased dramatically as *Roswell* fever has caught on. His popularity has sparked a loyal legion of fans who call themselves the "Fehrians" and monitor his every move on their respective websites. "Obviously, it's all worth something, because it tells you that you're doing a good job and that they like the show and appreciate what you're doing. But you have to draw the line. If [fan adulation is what] fulfills you as a person and makes you feel important, then you've got to give yourself a head check," Brendan has said.

Still, there's no doubt, his star *is* on the rise. Many have compared him to another "paranormal" TV star — David Duchovny. E! Online named Brendan one of their "Sizzling Sixteen" young stars to watch in 2000, comparing his on-screen intensity to that of the late movie star James Dean. The reference boggles Brendan's mind. "That's a huge compliment," Brendan told the popular entertainment website. "I'm a huge James Dean fan. But it's disrespectful to put me in his category."

The way his career is going, Brendan had better get used to the attention. "I'm very happy here, I like it, I've met great people, I like what I do," Brendan enthuses. "It's my time right now, and I'm really enjoying it. But I was *supposed* to be a teacher."

BRENDAN'S BEAT

FULL NAME: —————————— Brendan Fehr

HOW YOU SAY IT: —————————— "fair"

BIRTHDAY: —————————— October 29, 1977

ASTROLOGICAL SIGN: —————————— Scorpio

BIRTHPLACE: —————————— New Westminster, British Columbia, Canada

RAISED IN: ———— Winnipeg, Manitoba, Canada

FAMILY: —————————— Mom, Dad, two sisters

EDUCATION: —————————— Graduated from Mennonite Brethren Collegiate Institute (high school) in 1995

PETS: —————————— Dog, Opa, a rottweiler

HOBBIES: ———— Hockey, video games, sleeping

COMPARED TO: ——— James Dean, David Duchovny

FAVORITE SNACK: —————————— Fruity Pebbles

TASTEBUD BUMMER: ——— When Brendan misbehaved as a young boy, his mother would make him stick out his tongue — then she'd drip some Tabasco sauce on it.

UPCOMING PROJECT: ——— The movie *Final Destination* with Devon Sawa and Kerr Smith

MEET KATHERINE HEIGL

ISABEL EVANS

Beautiful Isabel Evans is a teen alien with sophisticated style and a saucy attitude. Sister to Max, Isabel is tall, blond, bold, and exudes confidence. Unlike Max and Michael, Isabel isn't afraid to use her powers whenever she feels like it. With a swipe of her hand, Isabel can change the colors of her lipstick, or make stains disappear from her clothing. And when she's in the mood for a little Foo Fighters or Bush, she holds a CD up to her ears and *voilà!* — she can rock in digital stereo! Neat trick!

While Isabel can be a definite "button-pushing, don't-stand-in-my-way" type of teen, she also has a warm, tender loving side. She's very close to Max and their "earth" family, especially her mom. Like Max and Michael, she wants to explore her mysterious past. But perhaps more than Max and Michael, it's Isabel who embraces the love and acceptance she experiences in Roswell. Katherine says of her character, "She's got many sides. She wants to fit in, she wants to be normal, and she doesn't want to have to be afraid."

Actress Katherine "Katie" Heigl certainly can relate to Isabel's longing to be "normal." When she was a teenager like Isabel, Katie longed to fit in with her classmates at New Canaan High School in New Canaan, Connecticut. "Because I was different — I was off doing movies and modeling and other stuff — I wasn't part of the popular crowd, so it was hard to deal with that. And it's one of those things that adults trivialize, but to kids — it's life or death."

In order to "fit in," Katie made a decision to put her burgeoning acting and modeling career on hold as much as possible until after she graduated. "The most important thing I realized was, in my sophomore year in high school, what sort of person I *wanted* to be, not what I *thought* I should be. And from then on it was on my terms. I made the best friends of my life that year, who are still my best friends."

THE BEGINNING

If Katie seems confident about what she wants in life, it could be due to her early childhood years. Katie was born in Washington, D.C., on November 24, 1978, to Nancy and John Heigl. Soon after her birth, the family relocated to the sprawling, affluent neighborhood of New Canaan, Connecticut. The tree-lined streets, green lawns, and excellent public schools provided the perfect setting for John and Nancy to raise their family, which also included Katie's two older siblings, John and Margaret.

Holidays at the Heigl home were — and still are — a slice right out of a Norman Rockwell painting. "We have wonderful family traditions," Katie explains. "My mom is an amazing cook and an amazing decorator. She goes all out at Christmas and brings out the Christmas village and the tree. We had this big old farmhouse in Connecticut, and we had two trees — one was smaller that Mom decorated in gold ornaments and we called it the gold tree."

On Christmas Eve, many friends and close relatives would gather at the Heigl house to celebrate the season. "Mom would have a huge dessert party, and she would make tons of really amazing desserts and Christmas cookies. We try to continue that every year."

Mom's creativity inspired young, blond-haired Katie to make her own holiday contributions. "I'm a big poetry writer. I love to write poetry for gifts because my family has always treated that like it's such a special gift. One year I made my father a scarf and I made my sister a very basic quilt, and I think I made bookmarks for everybody's stockings."

Halloween was yet another occasion for Katie to express herself. She loved dressing up in costumes and trick-or-treating around the neighborhood with her childhood pals. "My mother used to always help me with my Halloween costumes, so I always had these elaborate things. Once I was a princess and

I had this little dress and a little tiara. My mother put a mole on my upper lip."

Perhaps Katie's Halloween adventures were an early dress rehearsal for what would come next.

SMILE FOR THE CAMERAS

When Katie was nine, an aunt sent snapshots of her to a modeling agency — they immediately signed the photogenic young girl. Soon after, Katie was posing in flyers for stores like Sears and Lord & Taylor and doing commercials in nearby New York City. Instantly, Katie felt something had clicked inside of her. "It was like that was the thing for me. I really wanted to do it, and my mother was totally supportive," Katie explains.

The more Katie modeled, the more in demand she became. The one-hour train rides from New Canaan to New York City became a regular jaunt for mother and daughter and proved to be a real bonding experience. Even to this day, Katie enthuses, "My mom is my best friend. We get along so well, and she was such a tremendous support and influence in my life."

And thanks to her mother's encouragement and willingness to allow her daughter to follow her heart, Katie's modeling career expanded into the feature film world. *That Night,* which starred C. Thomas Howell and Juliette Lewis, was Katie's first film role. She was eleven. It was followed by the Depression-era drama *King of the Hill.*

French actor Gérard Depardieu played Katie's father in the 1994 feature *My Father, the Hero.* It was a big film for fourteen-year-old Katie and a personal turning point — her first on-screen kiss with actor Dalton James was her first kiss ever. Katie says the awkwardness of the situation was intensified because her mother was on the set. She told *Cosmo Girl,* "I was fourteen and he was twenty-two and *beautiful.* He asked, 'Have you ever French-kissed before? Because the director wants to make it look real.' And I was *horrified.*"

Luckily, Katie managed to get through that situation, and the film received solid reviews. She soon found herself playing the daughter of another superstar actor, Steven Segal, in the feature film *Under Siege 2.* That movie was a box office smash and young Katie got solid notices. Jay Leno asked her to appear on *The Tonight Show* to demonstrate some of the martial arts skills she'd learned from working with Mr. Segal.

Seventeen magazine jumped at the chance to put the young Hollywood sensation on their cover. It was a magical time for the high school sophomore, but back in New Canaan, it was business as usual. "When I would come back home from doing movies I was a normal kid going to school, doing my homework, hanging out with my friends."

But clearly, Katie was poised for stardom in a big way. While she was having fun with her blossoming career, she was also becoming interested in boys. One weekend on a trip to New York with her mother, Katie met actor Joey Lawrence (*Blossom*), and the two began a long-distance relationship that lasted nearly three months. Things might have blossomed into something more meaningful, but being on opposite coasts — Joey in California and Katie in Connecticut — made the relationship difficult to sustain.

The acting gigs kept coming for Katie, who tried to remain as normal as possible at her high school. During her junior and senior years, she landed roles in two more high-profile movies, *Wish Upon a Star* and *Bride of Chucky.* Going on location for these films meant long hours for Katie, who had to squeeze in her schoolwork around her shooting schedule. "My tutors on the set would work with my regular teachers in school. They would fax things back and forth to each other," Katie explains.

"I REALLY FELT I WANTED A SHOT"

In 1996 Katie's parents divorced, and in 1997, soon after Katie graduated from New Canaan High School, she and mom Nancy moved to Los Angeles. Katie is still very close with her father, who now works as a

Jason and Shiri as Max and Liz — their love
should never be.

Jason Behr

Life before *Roswell*: Jason, back row, right, was in TV's *Push* — a show that didn't last very long.

Shiri Appleby

Perfect Family was the name of Shiri's pre-*Roswell* TV show — it tanked.

Brendan Fehr

One of Brendan's first TV appearances was in the teleflick *Our Guys: Outrage in Glen Ridge*. He's the second guy on the right.

Majandra Delfino

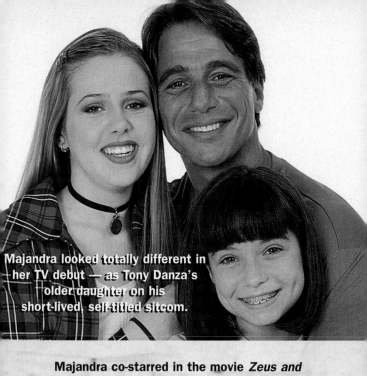

Majandra looked totally different in her TV debut — as Tony Danza's older daughter on his short-lived, self-titled sitcom.

Majandra co-starred in the movie *Zeus and Roxanne* with Miko Hughes and Jessica Howell.

Katherine Heigl

Katherine co-starred in the movie *My Father the Hero* back in 1995.

She went period-piece in TV's *The Tempest*.

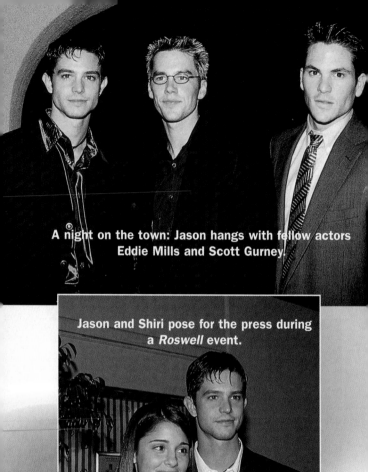

A night on the town: Jason hangs with fellow actors Eddie Mills and Scott Gurney.

Jason and Shiri pose for the press during a *Roswell* event.

Majandra dotes on her pooch Gertrude.

Majandra and Brendan are buds off-camera, too.

Colin Hanks

Yes, Colin is actor Tom Hanks' son — and yes, he is dating *Freaks & Geeks'* Busy Phillips.

Brendan Fehr

Jason Behr

banker in Washington, D.C. Of the decision to move west, she says, "After I graduated I had the choice of going to college or going to L.A., and I picked L.A. because I really felt I wanted a shot [at an acting career]."

What Katie knew in her heart soon became a reality after she and Nancy set up house in sunny Southern California. And just as she embraced the sandy beaches and palm trees of her new home, Hollywood casting directors embraced Katie. She landed parts in several small films and projects, including the TV movie *The Tempest* with Peter Fonda.

Katie feels it's no coincidence that she's worked with some of the most revered talents in Hollywood. Unlike many actors who are just happy to be working, Katie says she chooses her projects very carefully. "I have some basic questions I ask myself about a script and a character. What does this character have to say? Where is it going? What is it trying to get across? And the next questions are, who would I be working with? Who can I learn from?"

When Katie got called in to audition for

Roswell, she was instantly drawn to the project. "I was really excited about it. I thought the concept was really interesting. It adds the sci-fi theme to high school, but it also plays on the idea that everyone, at one time or another, feels like an alien in high school. Feels out of place, like they don't fit in. So I really like that they're drawing on that."

Originally Katie read for the leading role of Liz Parker. But the producers must have detected an otherworldly quality to Katie and had her return to read for Isabel. The feeling was mutual. "I wanted to be the alien!" Katie exclaims. "Isabel has this secret, it's like a disease, and she just wants to be treated like a normal human being."

But neither Katie nor her portrayal of Isabel could be classified as "normal." The extraordinary young actress has become a treat to watch each week on the hit show. And Katie couldn't be happier. "I'm having so much fun right now. I can't imagine doing anything else."

KATHERINE'S KORNER

FULL NAME: ——————— Katherine Heigl

HOW YOU SAY IT: ——————— HIGH-goal

NICKNAME: ——————— Katie

BIRTHDAY: ——————— November 24, 1978

ASTROLOGICAL SIGN: ——————— Sagittarius

BIRTHPLACE: ——————— Washington, D.C.

RAISED IN: ——————— New Canaan, Connecticut

FAMILY: ——————— Mom, Nancy, her manager

Dad, Paul, a banker

Brother, John

Sister, Margaret

EDUCATION: — Graduated from New Canaan High

School in 1997

PETS: ——————— Two miniature schnauzer dogs,

Anna and Romeo

HOBBIES: ——————— Kickboxing, yoga, drawing

FAVORITE FOOD: ——————— Sushi

FAVORITE BOOK: —*Prince of Tides* by Pat Conroy

MEET MAJANDRA DELFINO

MARIA DELUCA

Playing sassy, saucy waitress Maria DeLuca isn't much of a stretch for Majandra Delfino. "I have a very hot-blooded family, we're all Latin. I take bits and pieces of things we all do and it's really funny. We're a little overexcited. And I take all these excitable reactions that I see every day and I put them in Maria."

Maria is best friends with Liz Parker. The two are virtually inseparable — they eat lunch together in the school cafeteria, they socialize, and they work at the Crashdown Cafe. Oh yes, *and* they're both attracted to aliens! The friends complement each other very well — while Liz is soft, sweet, and shy, Maria is bold, brassy, and opinionated.

Majandra once said, "When someone is headstrong and gutsy, I am immediately attracted." So it's no wonder she can relate to her television alter ego. Maria is definitely someone who likes a challenge, which could explain why she fell for Michael. Her tell-it-like-it-is personality is enough to humanize the brooding, semi-social alien Michael. "My character is the most realistic," Majandra says. "Everyone else kind of takes the [alien] information in stride, while she is the one who acts the most human, as in *freaking out*. I think anyone in that circumstance would freak out." While Maria and Michael aren't a dating couple, their platonic relationship has provided for some very passionate on-screen romantic tension.

EARLY DAYS

Majandra's ability to emote passion stems from her loving family upbringing. She is the younger of two daughters born to a Venezuelan father and a Cuban-American mother in Caracas, Venezuela. Her real birth name is Maria Alejandra, but when her older sister, Marieh (MAR-EE-ay), had trouble pronouncing it, she created the nickname Majandra (Muh-HAND-dra), which has stuck ever since.

And Majandra the person, her family soon discovered, was turning out to be as unique as her nickname. When the tiny blond-haired tyke was three, the family moved to Miami, Florida. By then, Majandra was already entertaining her family, singing and dancing to songs she'd hear on the radio.

She was a natural born performer, and her mother, Mary, was proud of her young daughter's talents. She enrolled her in ballet lessons, then acting, singing, and piano lessons. The tiny tot's schedule was power-packed with activities, and she couldn't have been happier. It seemed like whatever Majandra tried, she was good at. When she wasn't belting out a tune or twirling in a tutu, Majandra enjoyed going to the beach and swimming; ice-skating; and hanging out with big sis Marieh and her friends.

Thanks to her supportive family, which now included a new stepdad (her parents split when she was young), Majandra was able to satisfy her appetite for performing. They encouraged her to explore her artistic side and took pride whenever she performed, whether it was at home or in school plays like *Peter Pan.* As Majandra's talents expanded, so did her audiences. Soon she branched out into local community theater productions of *Grease* and *Oliver.* When she was ten, she landed a prestigious role as a dancer in *The Nutcracker* with the Miami Ballet.

SCHOOL DAYS

At the same time as she was excelling in extracurricular performing, Majandra saw her usually high grades decline. "I went through lower school getting good grades, and then in the fifth grade, I started doing badly. My parents were, like, 'Now, you have to do your homework,' and I remember it was impossible. It was so not routine. I had to go back and relearn everything."

Majandra's parents recognized that their daughter needed a little help focusing on her schoolwork, so they hired a tutor. "They put me together with a tutor and made sure I could do all this because I was always doing so well," Majandra explains. "What happened was up until the fourth grade, they put me in advanced math, and I wasn't really ready for it. In fifth grade is when it became impossible for me to keep up, and that is where I started getting frustrated. I still hate doing homework. But it definitely made a difference."

Majandra's determination to get her grades back on track (which she did) equaled her passion to perform. The bilingual Majandra became a huge fan of the Latin music scene, which was thriving in Miami long before it became a mainstream success in the late '90s.

One of Majandra's best friends back then was a young girl named Samantha Gibb, whose father is Maurice Gibb of the legendary pop/disco group the Bee Gees. The two girls shared a love of poetry, songwriting, and singing, and became fast friends — and collaborators. They formed a singing group called China Doll and began performing around town. A highlight came when the Bee Gees were performing a benefit concert at Miami's Fountainbleau Hotel and asked the girls if they'd like to open for them. Naturally, they accepted, and the evening was a magical experience for Majandra.

"THEY GAVE ME SIX MONTHS TO TRY IT"

While Majandra and Samantha continued to write, perform, and record, Majandra's ever-growing interests in the arts expanded toward acting. Her parents wanted to be supportive of their daughter's yearning desires, but at the same time, they were skeptical about the whole "Hollywood scene."

"I was fourteen at the time, and we were living in Miami, and I really wanted to try acting," Majandra explains. "So my mother said, 'Okay, you have six months to try this. But you have to book something *big*.'"

Nothing like a little pressure! Majandra

knew that her parents wanted her to be happy and challenged and fulfilled, but at the same time they were worried that "the business" of Hollywood would be a negative environment for their daughter. It was their way of telling her that if she really wanted it, she'd have to give it her all. Majandra decided to go after acting with the same zeal that she'd applied to the other important things in her life — schoolwork, music, and dancing.

READY, SET, GO!

With the parentally imposed time limit set, Majandra had her work cut out for her. A local Miami talent agency signed the fourteen-year-old, and within three months, she landed one of the lead roles in the feature film *Zeus and Roxanne.* That totally qualified as "big." The decision to forge ahead on the film seemed like a no-brainer, with one exception — school. Majandra had been accepted to New World School of the Arts, Miami's prestigious performing arts high school. Ironically, she couldn't do both — attend that school *and* go away on location for the movie. After discussing the pros and cons of each scenario with her family, Majandra decided to stick with her regular school, and have a tutor.

Majandra played a feisty teenager named Judith opposite actress Kathleen Quinlan (*Apollo 13*), who played her mother Mary Beth. Her real-life parents, who had been skeptical of the business, now felt more at ease with their daughter's career path. "My mom was pretty supportive after that," Majandra says with a giggle. "I know I'm pretty lucky because things don't normally happen that fast."

Majandra had lots of fun on the family-oriented movie about how a friendship between a dolphin and a dog ignites a romance between their respective owners. The film was shot in the Bahamas, not too far from Majandra's home. But she also learned the downside of being an actress. "It was really exciting, but not at all what I expected. It wasn't glamorous," Majandra says bluntly. "It required waking up at four in the morning almost every day, and it ruined the whole aspect of seeing movies and believing them for me."

So maybe the illusion of Hollywood storytelling was stripped away, but the reality of being a working actress remained appealing. Not long after *Zeus and Roxanne* wrapped, the budding star was called out to Los Angeles to audition for several producers who were developing new television shows. Once again, Majandra landed a lead role — this time on a new NBC comedy, *The Tony Danza Show.* Her own family decided to set up house in Los Angeles (they kept their Miami digs, too), and Majandra began the arduous task of balancing schoolwork and a weekly television series.

Majandra played Tony's rebellious daughter Tina DiMeo. The role was very appealing. Majandra explained at the time, "Tina is a very emotional, strong-willed girl with a good head on her shoulders, and she's definitely not naive."

Tony was very popular with television audiences thanks to his prior roles in *Taxi* and

Who's the Boss? It looked like Majandra's television debut would be on a show that had all the makings of a hit — a big name star, a big name network, and a talented writing staff. But the show, which premiered in fall 1997, received mixed reviews and less than desirable ratings. It was canceled that December.

Disappointed, sure. But down-and-out? Not Majandra. She and the family continued to split time between Los Angeles and Miami, and Majandra continued to land guest television roles on shows like *Sabrina, the Teenage Witch*. On the feature film front, she appeared in *I Know What You Screamed Last Summer* (a spoof on the teen horror flick that starred Jennifer Love Hewitt), *The Secret Lives of Girls* (a coming-of-age drama that starred Linda Hamilton), and *The Learning Curve*.

In early 1999, months before she graduated from high school, Majandra got the call to audition for the producers of *Roswell*. The show instantly appealed to her — as did her new friends. "Everyone in this cast is crazy!"

Majandra announces. "I have the best time at work, and we all like each other and get along."

Majandra is deep into *Roswell*, but she hasn't abandoned her musical roots. The nineteen-year-old actress is still plugging away, writing, singing, and recording in hopes of landing a still-elusive record deal. "Acting for me is like a fun job," Majandra said recently.

MAJANDRA MINUTIAE

FULL NAME: —————— Maria Alejandra Delfino

NICKNAME: ————— Majandra (Muh-HAHN-druh), given to her by older sister Marieh

BIRTHDAY: —————— February 20, 1981

ASTROLOGICAL SIGN: —————— Pisces

BIRTHPLACE: —————— Caracas, Venezuela

RAISED IN: ——— Miami, Florida, and Los Angeles, California

FAMILY: —————————— Mom, Mary
Stepdad, Leopoldo
Sister, Marieh

EDUCATION: ———————— Graduated from high school in 1999

PETS: ———————— Gertrude, a standard poodle
Tattoo, a Pekingese

HOBBIES: ———————— Shopping, music

SNACKS ON: ———— Reese's Peanut Butter Cups

FAVORITE TV SHOW: ———————— *Charmed*

FAVORITE MOVIE: ———————— *The Last Unicorn*

MUSICAL TASTES: ———————— Björk, Portishead

ADVICE TO TEENS: ———————— "Be happy with being you."

MEET COLIN HANKS

ALEX WHITMAN

Colin Hanks's character, Alex Whitman, is the kind of friend everyone should have. He's kind and thoughtful, mild mannered and polite. Best of all, he's loyal. Soon after the shooting incident at the Crashdown Cafe, Alex discovered that Liz and Maria had been keeping a secret from him. He asked Maria for the truth — and when she told him that their new "friends" were aliens, he stammered and stuttered with amazement — but vowed to keep the secret.

Even though Alex is the same age as his friends, he seems a little naive — especially when it comes to male-female relationships. Colin says this aspect of his character's personality is most like his own.

"Being shy, especially with girls, that's definitely me," Colin says.

What else does he have in common with his character? "There's a lot of me in Alex. I wouldn't necessarily say I'm a really funny guy, but I do tend to have moments where at least I crack *myself* up — and I think Alex does that to himself a lot. In terms of being this really easygoing sort of goofball, that's definitely me."

CHIP OFF THE OLD BLOCK

The first question Colin is invariably asked when people meet him is the obvious: "Are you related to Tom Hanks?" The answer is yes — Colin is Tom's son. But when Colin was born in November 1978, it was years before his father, a two-time Academy Award–winning actor, would make it big.

So much for the assumption that Colin was born with a silver spoon in his mouth. At the time of his son's birth, Tom was a struggling, unknown stage actor living in a cockroach-infested apartment in a rough

New York City neighborhood. He was twenty-two and barely had a cent to his name. Because work was so hard to find, Tom was collecting unemployment checks.

Struggling to make a name for himself and support his new wife and son, Tom landed a role on the ABC sitcom *Bosom Buddies* in 1980. The show was about two grown men in the advertising industry who dress as women so that they can live in an affordable female-only dormitory. Two days after Colin's second birthday, *Bosom Buddies* debuted.

Who would have guessed that twenty years later, Colin would make *his* television debut? And even more ironic, *Roswell* is filmed on the same Paramount Studios lot where *Bosom Buddies* was made.

With his career taking off, Tom moved the family, which now included Colin's little sister, Elizabeth, to sunny Los Angeles. No more cockroaches and cold winter nights. Instead, Colin and Elizabeth enjoyed playing in their new backyard with lots of toys. Dad had finally made it and was able to support the family the way he always wanted to. After two seasons, *Bosom Buddies* was canceled. Tom moved into films, working on hits like *Splash* and *Bachelor Party*.

Sadly, life at home was falling apart. Colin's parents' marriage was breaking up, and no matter what they tried to do, they couldn't save it. Tom feared that his kids would have trouble growing up away from their father. But he vowed to be there for them whenever they needed him. And even more important, he vowed to make their childhoods as normal as possible. Soon after the divorce was final, Colin, his mother, and Elizabeth moved to Sacramento, California.

GROWING UP NORMAL

What's "normal"? For Colin, it was life in suburbia. Sacramento, California, is a city located at the opposite end of the state from Los Angeles. "Normal" was life *away* from the business of Hollywood and movies and paparazzi. Colin could have easily grown up to be a spoiled brat like many kids whose parents are in show business. But because of his parents' commitment to raising him and his sister with solid family and moral values, Colin is as "normal" a twenty-two-year-old as a parent could wish for.

Colin had household responsibilities like taking out the trash and keeping his room neat. From an early age, academics were always stressed. Colin and Elizabeth learned to develop their own interests and hobbies. That doesn't mean that Colin wasn't curious about what his father was up to. In fact, even though it might have been easy for Tom to snap his fingers and get Colin acting work, he didn't. Instead, he let Colin develop on his own. When he was a young boy, Colin explains, "I played with a lot of toys, that basically consisted of my acting."

But by the time he became a teenager, Colin joined the drama club and got into junior high and high school productions.

Tom Hanks saw his son's potential to become a chip off the old block. "I remember seeing him in shows in junior high school and I thought, 'Oh, he's got the chops,'" the star told columnist Marilyn Beck.

In addition to his growing passion for acting, the six feet two inches Colin became an avid sports fan, a passion he shared with his mom, Samantha. "When the San Jose Sharks started playing in the NHL (National Hockey League) their first year, they played in San Francisco," Colin recalls. "My mom bought me a season package of ten games, and every day of the game she'd pick me up from school and we'd drive to the Bay Area from Sacramento and watch the games. And then she'd drive back home while I was asleep or doing my homework," Colin explains, noting with a grin, "I always opted for sleep because I never wanted to do my homework. That was one of the coolest things I ever did with her."

Colin continued to explore his interests throughout high school, but it was clear acting was foremost on his mind. During breaks from school, he visited his father on the sets of movies like *Apollo 13* and *That Thing You Do*. In fact, Colin's first professional acting credit was in *That Thing You*

Do. But because education was a priority, Colin packed his suitcase and headed off to college right after graduating from high school.

Colin enrolled at Loyola Marymount University in Los Angeles in the fall of 1996. "I majored in theater," he explains, noting that he didn't complete the required studies to earn a degree. But he did hone his acting skills there. Colin was a featured player in some of LMU's productions, including the comedy *Noises Off!*

"I GOTTA TAKE IT"

It certainly didn't hurt to have the last name Hanks when Colin began looking for a professional agent. But as any producer or director will tell you, connections will only get you so far. If you don't have talent, you won't last long in Hollywood. However, as his dad recognized, Colin had the chops. After a series of auditions in 1998, Colin had a weekend he won't ever forget. One Friday afternoon he got a call from his agent that he'd landed the part of Cosmo, a quirky friend, in the teen romantic comedy *Whatever It Takes.* That following Monday, just as Colin was about to report to work on the film, his agent called again. He'd been cast as Alex in *Roswell!*

"I got this opportunity and I said 'All right, I gotta take it.' So here I am," Colin says humbly. He knows how competitive the industry can be, and he's grateful to have a shot at his own career. But if it were all over tomorrow, Colin wouldn't worry. He's got other performing aspirations up his sleeve. "I would be a musician. I play the bass guitar, so if I couldn't do acting, then I'd probably try to take a crack at playing bass professionally." But, he adds wryly, "I don't know if I'd be nearly as successful."

The way things look, Colin won't have to sing for his supper anytime soon. And as for dad, the worries he might have had when Colin was young seem to have dissipated. He's at ease knowing that Colin is following in his footsteps as long as it's what his son really wants to do. "I want all of my kids to develop some passion for what they do, so it doesn't seem like work when they do it," Tom told Marilyn Beck. "And that he's been able to pursue that and actually land a gig — well, I'm ludicrously proud of him."

CODE ON COLIN

FULL NAME: ———————————— Colin Hanks

BIRTHDAY: ——————————— November 24, 1978

ASTROLOGICAL SIGN: ————————— Sagittarius

BIRTHPLACE: ———————— New York, New York

RAISED IN: ————— New York, New York, and
Sacramento, California

FAMILY: ———————— Dad, actor Tom Hanks
Mom, actress Samantha Lewes
Sister, Elizabeth
Half brothers, Chester and Truman

EDUCATION: —— Graduated from high school in
1997. Studied theater at Loyola Marymount University in Los Angeles, California

FAVE TV SHOWS: —— *The Simpsons, Freaks and Geeks, Dennis Miller Live, The Chris Rock Show*

FAVE FOOD: —— "I'll eat anything. I'm not worried about my figure."

SPACE FANTASY:—"If I lived like the Jetsons, my room could be a mess and my robot maid would pick everything up. That would be fun."

HOBBIES:————————— Plays bass guitar

UPCOMING PROJECTS:——— *Whatever It Takes* with Shane West (*Once and Again*), Marla Sokoloff (*The Practice*), and James Franco (*Freaks and Geeks*)

MEET NICK WECHSLER

KYLE VALENTI

Poor Kyle Valenti. His girlfriend Liz Parker dumped him for another guy, his dad is the town sheriff, and to add insult to injury, he recently injured his leg in a Roswell Comets basketball game. Kyle is a stereotypical handsome school jock, a strong silent type who struts his stuff in his high school letterman jacket. He'll never wear his heart on his sleeve, but deep down inside that brooding tough-guy exterior is a sensitive young man.

Nick Wechsler says it's fun to play Kyle because they have at least some things in common. "I think I would have a similar reaction to being dumped by a woman," Nick says of Kyle and Liz's relationship. "I don't really see a huge difference between him and me other than he's a cowboy and I'm not."

Nick is actually kidding about the cowboy reference — he grew up in cowboy country, Albuquerque, New Mexico. Like Kyle, he loves sports. "I did wrestling, which is funny to me because I think that's the one thing left that they could do on the show. That's the only sport I really know how to do. There was an episode where I was supposed to be playing basketball and I have no idea how to play basketball and we spent all day setting up the shots so I look like I know how to play. I stunk up the joint so bad, they ended up using like a minute of the thing in the show! I'm, like, please, let's do something with wrestling. I can look like I know what I'm doing with that!"

HOME ON THE RANGE

Nick was the fifth of eight sons born to Janet, an administrative assistant for the U.S. Forest Service, and Joseph, a sheet metal worker. It's no wonder Nick excelled at sports, especially wrestling. There's nothing like a household full of boys to keep everybody on their game, so to speak. But the sibling rivalry took a back seat to the brotherly love in the Wechsler house.

Albuquerque is located in central New Mexico, approximately two hundred miles from Roswell. This beautiful desert country is bordered by the majestic Sandia Mountain Range and is home to the world-famous Kodak International Hot Air Balloon Festival, which takes place every October. Many people there are involved in cattle ranching or farming. It's also a rich cultural center with a large Navajo population whose traditions are reflected in the city's architecture, food, and arts. Nick speaks fondly of his New Mexican roots. "In Albuquerque I didn't ever feel I had a problem finding nice people or nice places."

In junior high school and later at Highland High School, Nick excelled at wrestling. "It was really exciting learning and everything," he says of the difficult sport. But one day, while attending a school play, Nick had a brainstorm. "I saw a play in high school in, like, tenth grade, it was *Tartuffe*, and it was terrible," Nick recalls. "I thought everybody in it was really bad, and I was, like, 'I can do this.'"

Perhaps it was Nick's innate competitive nature or the fact that he had truly found his calling. Or maybe he was inspired by other Albuquerque natives who've made it big — Freddie Prinze, Jr., Neil Patrick Harris, and French Stewart. Whatever the case, Nick decided to give acting a try. "That feeling of '*I* can do this and I'm no one,'" Nick explains. "Honestly, that's still driving me. I just wanted to show everybody. There were kids who thought they were hilarious and that kind of thing drove me crazy. I liked the idea of them realizing they're not as great as they thought they were."

Nick also liked the fact that he was a natural on the stage. "I joined drama and I was in almost every production after that. I'd like to think I did pretty well."

Nick's drama teacher also felt her student was a gifted young actor and encouraged him to enroll in a school-sponsored film acting workshop. "That's kind of what got me thinking about acting professionally," Nick says. In the summer of 1996, following his graduation from Highland High School, Nick moved to the bright lights and big city of Los Angeles to pursue his dream. "My mom and some of my brothers drove out here with me," Nick explains. "We went to Disneyland and they helped me find a place to live and then they left me. They had to go back."

Nick was excited by the prospect of being a professional actor but sad about leaving his family and friends behind. Los Angeles is a concrete jungle full of traffic-jammed freeways and, more importantly, full of actors. It was a world away from Albuquerque and if Nick was going to make it, he'd have to give it all he had. "I kept telling myself if I didn't make it within a year I was going to quit and move back."

ROLL THE CREDITS

Luckily for Nick, things started to happen pretty quickly. With his self-imposed time constraint, Nick instantly immersed himself in the acting culture of L.A. He landed bit parts in television shows like *The Lazarus Man,* with Robert Urich, and *Silk Stalkings,* with Rob Estes. To supplement his sporadic acting gigs, Nick, who's also passionate about music, worked in a record store. "But not for long. [Success] happened pretty fast, but I had no experience so I didn't know what to expect. I guess I just assumed that's how it worked."

He also had a small role in the feature film *The Perfect Game* and almost was in the hit movie *American Beauty.* "But when I showed up to tape my part, I found out they were cutting costs, and my part was cut out," Nick explained to the *Albuquerque Journal.* He was especially disappointed because the movie stars one of his favorite actors of all time, Kevin Spacey. "Even though my part was small, it would have been great to have even one line in a movie with him."

But Nick wasn't bummed for long. In late 1998, Nick auditioned for and landed the role of Kyle on *Roswell.* Though he's never been to the real Roswell, Nick feels at home on the set with his new friends, the cast, and crew. "Working with Bill Sadler is amazing," Nick gushes of his TV dad. "I think he's great, not just as an actor but as a person. He's really friendly and I really enjoy his company outside of the show."

And even though he misses his family and friends from Albuquerque, Nick couldn't be happier with the way his career is going. "I've never been the biggest fan of California," Nick admits. "There are certain places that I like, but I feel like that is all so rare. I miss Albuquerque in some ways, but it's not really home anymore. I used to think I wanted to live there the rest of my life, and I moved out here to do this. I still love the place and all my favorite people in the world are there and it will always be really special. But I don't feel like I need to live there anymore."

NICK'S NOTES

FULL NAME: ———————— NICK WECHSLER
HOW YOU SAY IT: ——————————WEX-ler
BIRTHDAY: ————————— September 3, 1978
ASTROLOGICAL SIGN: ————————— Virgo

HEIGHT:———————————————— 5' 7"

BIRTHPLACE:———— Albuquerque, New Mexico

RAISED IN:————— Albuquerque, New Mexico

FAMILY:————————————— Mom, Janet

Dad, Joseph

Seven brothers (four older, three younger)

EDUCATION:— Graduated in 1996 from Highland

High School in Albuquerque, New Mexico

FAVE TV SHOW:————————*The X-Files*

FAVORITE FOOD:———————————— Gyros

HOBBIES:———— Learning to play acoustic guitar

9

BEHIND THE SCENES

There's a lot to see in *Roswell,* and not all of it takes place in front of the camera. Most of the show is filmed at *Roswell*'s home away from New Mexico, a soundstage on the legendary Paramount Studios lot in Hollywood, California.

Paramount is a studio rich with tradition that can be traced back to the early days of film and television. Located at 5555 Melrose Avenue, it was home to popular television shows like *Happy Days, Mork & Mindy,* and *Cheers.* Paramount is "just down the street" from famed Melrose Avenue's chic fashion boutiques and trendy restaurants. Today, the stars of *Roswell* drive through the same black wrought iron gates that actors like Ron Howard, Robin Williams, Ted Danson — and yes, Colin's dad, Tom Hanks — did years ago. The lot is also home for current TV hits like *Frasier* and *Star Trek Voyager.*

Roswell's set is comprised of several main soundstages, most notably the Crashdown Cafe and Roswell High School's classrooms, hallways, and lunch area. Depending on what's being shot, other makeshift sets like Max and Isabel's house, Sheriff Valenti's office, or Liz's bedroom can quickly be put in place. When the show needs an exterior location, like a school or nightclub, everyone goes to nearby Covina, California. And those contemplative dust bowl desert scenes where Max, Isabel, and Michael convene are sometimes shot in a popular hiking spot known as Vasquez Rocks.

While it's a common practice for half-hour sitcoms to tape in front of a live studio audience, *Roswell*'s set, like that of most dramas, is closed to the public. Only the cast, crew, and credentialed visitors can be on the lot. Each one-hour episode of *Roswell* takes approximately five to seven days to shoot. The reason the length of time varies is because sometimes different scenes require different settings. It's not that the *Roswell* folks wouldn't like to see their fans. But because they are under a time constraint to film a certain number of pages of the script each day, they can't afford any distractions, especially when they put in an average of fourteen to sixteen hours each day.

There's a catering department (also known as "craft services") on the set to make sure everyone is properly nourished. Breakfast, lunch, and dinner are served at regular hours. While the menu varies from day to day, a steady stream of chips, candies, sodas, coffee, and fruit is available to the cast and crew throughout the day. It's one of Colin's favorite places to be. Colin teases, "I just eat as many bratwursts as the catering guys will cook up for me, and I'll go back for seconds."

IN BETWEEN SCENES

A weekly television series requires the efforts of many people who work in front of and behind the camera. The actors are the ones who receive all of the praise, but in reality, they are just one component of many that go into making *Roswell* a success.

Most of the *Roswell* cast weren't strangers to movie and TV sets, Still, they say the biggest adjustment they've had to make is the long hours. Not all of the actors are required to work at the same time, because not every actor is in every scene. So someone might show up for work at eleven in the morning but not actually shoot his or her scheduled scene until three or four in the afternoon.

COLIN says one of his biggest adjustments to working on a TV series is, believe it or not, getting enough rest so that he's energized when it's time to work. In between scenes and during his downtime, Colin spends most of his time in his trailer, "sleeping, taking naps. I'm just starting to get into the concept of doing stuff while I'm not working. I'm slowly getting books here and there."

But it's hard to catch a wink on this active set. When he's not sleeping, Colin is usually mixing it up with the crew. "I talk a lot of shop about basketball with a lot of guys on the crew." Colin notes that he's a big Lakers fan. "I'm always up for talking a little hoops. We talk about the previous game, the next coming game, if there's a game on we try and watch."

Colin also enjoys playing WWF Smackdown on his new Color Game Boy. "It's one of those really old, cool games where the guys punch, punch, kick, kick. That's kind of fun," he says. And when he's in an introspective mood, "I keep a journal. That's pretty much the only downtime I have to really write."

Avid reader KATIE says she spends a lot of her downtime looking for her next book. "My friends and I are always saying, 'What have you read lately? What would be a good book to get?' I love to read fiction. So I'm always going through the *New York Times* best-seller list and the Oprah Book Club."

Mild-mannered SHIRI can be seen snapping photos of the cast and crew with her new digital camera. "I was into playing Sega for a while, but I started blinking and seeing Tetris in my eyes, so I gave that up," Shiri jokes. "I just got this camera and have gotten into photography, so I'm really enjoying that. I take a lot of random, goofing-around pictures on the set. Well, Majandra really plays it up for me. She gives me what I need. She and Brendan are really great with the camera. And the crew is so hysterical and so funny. They'll do anything."

When MAJANDRA isn't vamping it for Shiri's camera, she is usually cutting it up with Brendan or Nick, or hanging out with Katie. "We're just like little girls," Majandra gushed about Katie to *People* magazine. Shiri echoes Majandra's sentiments. "The gals just bonded right away." In fact, the entire cast bonded right away. That's why they feel so comfortable playfully teasing one another as they work. Majandra recalled one particularly funny moment to *16* magazine. "There was this hilarious scene when Michael throws Kyle, but he threw him so hard, Kyle went over the couch. All the cast was standing there laughing, but Nick just kept on acting until they called, 'Cut!'"

"Jason," Brendan told *TV Week,* "has a million impressions and a million accents which are really funny."

BRENDAN and his alien mate have forged a true friendship. "We're like the little boys in class laughing every time the teacher says something funny. Our sense of humor is so immature, we find absolutely anything funny," Brendan said recently.

And what about Brendan? "I get razzed about my accent," the Canadian actor sheepishly admitted to a reporter. "You let one 'eh' out or let slip one 'sorry' instead of 'sawry' and they're all over you! But it's all in good fun. I poke fun at them for being American, but I have to tread lightly because I'm surrounded by about a hundred of 'em every day."

In fact, you can count on Brendan, Jason, Katie, or Majandra to jump at any chance they get to playfully mock or imitate one another — always in the spirit of good, clean fun. Brendan also notes that a *Roswell* cast and crew poll would surely vote Nick the "funniest man ever."

When NICK isn't cracking up Brendan and Majandra, chances are he can be found strumming on an acoustic guitar in his trailer. "Bill Sadler gave me a guitar," Nick explains of his new six-string. "He collects them and he's a very good guitarist and musician — he plays a lot of acoustic blues and a lot of folksy stuff. I told him I wanted to learn how to play and he gave me an older guitar. It's kind of been around but I've never had one before."

While Nick is a huge music fan and has amassed a sizable CD collection thanks to his former job at a record store, he says that if you hear some rockin' tunes coming out of his trailer, chances are it *isn't* him. "I didn't know how to play before and I'm practicing now. But I don't think anyone should expect anything from me."

It's rare for a television show to have so much camaraderie and mutual admiration. Brendan still marvels at how lucky everyone is to be together. "It's kind of amazing that they take people from all corners of North America, and they stick 'em together, and they all get along so well."

Shiri adds that the cast's on-screen chemistry is definitely not just for show.

"We really like each other. We talk, we laugh, we celebrate each other's birthdays together. It's become this little family."

JASON, who's the oldest cast member, told a *New York Times* reporter, "This has been a lot of long hours, but it doesn't really seem like work because of the people I'm surrounded by every day. We've got a great cast, a great crew and great producers. The company I keep makes it fun and makes it a treat to be around here all the time."

Perhaps Shiri says it best. "Everyone is getting along so well and has become friends, it's such a warm, friendly environment. Having such great people there for you makes the process of making a show so much easier."

CHOW DOWN AT THE CRASHDOWN CAFE

Every show has a hangout, a central meeting place where the characters can congregate for good food and conversation. The friends of *Friends* have Central Perk, the kids of *Beverly Hills, 90210* have the Peach Pit, and the *Roswell* gang have the Crashdown Cafe.

Liz Parker's dad is the proprietor of the Crashdown, so no wonder she and best pal Maria act like they own the place. Oftentimes, Liz and Maria's personal problems take precedence over good customer service, though.

Life at the Crashdown can be pretty exciting at times, as evidenced by the shooting incident that first brought Liz and Max together. But more often than not, the cafe is crowded with lookie-loo tourists and locals competing to sit in one of its red vinyl booths. It's a place where Max, Michael, Isabel, and Alex can unwind after school, even if it means that Liz and Maria have to wait on them. They can socialize, do their algebra homework, and enjoy a slice of blackberry pie.

And for the traveling tourist who wants to take a piece of Roswell home, alien memorabilia, in the form of coffee mugs, T-shirts, postcards, and fake antennas, is available.

The bright orange walls, covered with overlapping martian-green triangles, give the diner an art deco feel. Of course the Crashdown Cafe is fictional. It's part of the *Roswell* set on the Paramount Studios lot in Hollywood. But any visitor would certainly be tempted to sit down for a meal. The cafe looks so realistic, right down to the cappuccino machine, amber drinking glasses, and cutlery on the tables.

SERVE IT UP

Making Liz and Maria's outfits as authentic and kitschy as possible was the job of *Roswell* costume designer Laura Goldsmith.

She says that she combined the standard vintage-style waitress uniform with a little bit of alien magic on top. The result was an aquamarine dress with a silver pleather collar and a matching silver pleather alien-head apron. To top it off, the waitresses wear silver bobbing antennae headpieces.

WHAT'S ON THE MENU?

All this diner talk sure does work up an appetite. And if you're hungry, the Crashdown is the place to be. And you won't go broke trying to fill your belly.

Take a look at what's available at the Crashdown. And remember, don't forget to tip your waitress!

DRINKS

Cosmic Cola $1.00

UFO/H2O $1.00

Abduct-Tea $1.00

GREEN MARTIAN SHAKE $1.00

CRASHSITE SHAKE $2.00

METEOR SHOWER MALT $2.00

BLOOD OF MARTIAN SMOOTHIE . . .$2.00

LUNAR SPECIALS

SEA SPACE PORT $2.00

SIGOURNEY WEAVER KICK-ALIEN

BURGER $3.00

WILL SMITH INNOCENT BYSTANDER

BURGER $3.00

GRILLED MOONCHEESE

SANDWICH AND ORBIT RINGS $2.50

SPACED OUT SOUP $1.00/CUP

. . . .$2.00/BOWL

SIDE DISHES

TOSSED ALIEN SALAD $2.00

UNIDENTIFIED FRENCH FRYING

OBJECT $1.00

INTERPLANETARY PICKLES .75 CENTS EACH

DESSERT   (ask your server for prices)

MEN IN BLACKBERRY PIE

HOT FUDGE BLAST-OFF SUNDAE

DO YOU BELIEVE?

It's been more than fifty years since citizens of Roswell, New Mexico, reported seeing an unidentified flying object fall from the sky. On July 3, 1947, witnesses told police what they saw. In July 1997, the *Albuquerque Journal* newspaper printed a series of eyewitness accounts to mark the golden anniversary. The story began, "Since the summer day a half century ago that Corona rancher Mac Brazel went on horseback to check on his sheep and found the remains of something that had crashed from the sky, things haven't really been the same."

No, things haven't been the same, in Roswell, or anywhere else for that matter. The reported crash that so many people "thought" they saw, the government explained days later on July 9, 1947, was actually an experimental weather balloon that had fallen from the sky. The U.S. government quickly gathered the fallen debris, then dismissed the blow-by-blow accounts of farmers, Navajo Indians, and other citizens of central New Mexico. But could all these people have possibly imagined the same thing?

"The Roswell Incident," as it has become known, sparks as much debate today as it did in 1947. Were there truly "dipping discs" seen in the clear New Mexico sky that evening? Or is it a legend? Was there a government coverup?

What is true is that the events that unfolded that summer caused mortals around the world to raise the question, 'Are we alone?'

HOLLYWOOD BELIEVES

While the U.S. government would just as soon bury the theories of life on other planets, the fertile imaginations of Hollywood television and film producers keep the vision alive. Steven Spielberg raised eyebrows when he directed the blockbuster hits *Close Encounters of the Third Kind* and *E.T.*

Television shows like *Star Trek*, *Lost in Space*, and *My Favorite Martian* hammed up the notion that there was life beyond Earth. But thought-provoking projects such as television's *The X-Files* and the feature film *Contact* are proof that people still believe, as *The X-Files'* motto goes, "The truth is out there."

SURVEY SAYS?

So what do the stars of *Roswell* have to say about the alien controversy? Do they believe in UFOs? Is there life on other planets?

JASON BEHR

"*E.T.* had a profound impact on me when I was a child. I really enjoyed movies with this subject matter. *Star Wars* was one of my favorite movies. The whole trilogy was a major part of my upbringing. I think that the fantasy and the discovery of it all and the idea behind the fact that there could be other intelligent life-forms out there is fascinating. For me to sit up here and tell you that *we* are the only intelligent life-form that ever existed would be very arrogant of me. To be honest, I don't know. We are just one speck in a grander scale. It feels if there wasn't anybody else out there, it would be a bit disappointing. It would be a bit lonely."

SHIRI APPLEBY

"I wasn't a believer in aliens or UFOs before the show, but working on the show I see so much stuff and I think it's hard not to believe. You've got to have some kind of belief that maybe 'something' might exist. It would be pretty naive of us to think we're the only kind of creatures out there."

BRENDAN FEHR

"I definitely believe in the possibility."

"I think there must be life out there. I just don't know which planets and where. Everyone always assumes aliens would be dangerous, that they'd be out to hurt us. I just think they'd be out to learn from us, or we would learn from them. To interact with other beings, I think it would be cool. And do I believe in aliens? Dennis Rodman, maybe."

MAJANDRA DELFINO

"I really have the most faith in aliens because I believe there is no doubt. I have theories like every sci-fi fan. I never had an experience, it's just one of those things where you kind of look at the world and think. When I was little, I looked at the world and thought, 'I can't believe these people are almost so self-centered in a way. That they think they're the only people in the universe. And everything revolves around Earth, like we're the only life.' I always thought, 'Come on, there has to be something else out there, and people are just being naive or keeping us naive.'"

COLIN HANKS

"I believe. I'm the one most likely to step into the cantina scene in *Star Wars.* I liked *Star Wars* as much as the next guy. It's something fun to believe in, that's for sure. It's like in that movie *Contact*: 'It would be a whole lot of wasted space if there's no one else around.' Whether aliens are going to be coming down and talking with us any time soon I really have no idea. I hope so. That would be interesting."

NICK WECHSLER

"Call me crazy, but I believe in UFOs."

WEBSITES AND ADDRESSES

Can't get enough of *Roswell*? There are plenty of cyber shrines to the show on the Internet. For the latest in *Roswell* episode rundowns, cast bios, and links to other WB programs, go to the official website, **www.thewb.com**

As an added bonus, Jason Behr has his own official website, **www.jasonbehr.com**

Snail mail can be sent to any of the *Roswell* gang at the following address:

Roswell
Warner Bros. Television Network
4000 Warner Boulevard
Burbank, CA 91522

HEY CARSON!
MEET TRL'S CARSON DALY

Hey fans — here is everything you want to know about Carson Daly, MTV's most popular VJ and the host of *Total Request Live*. Packed with photos, facts, and personal quotes from Carson Daly, this super biography gives you THE inside scoop on MTV's hottest star!

Catch it this June wherever books are sold!